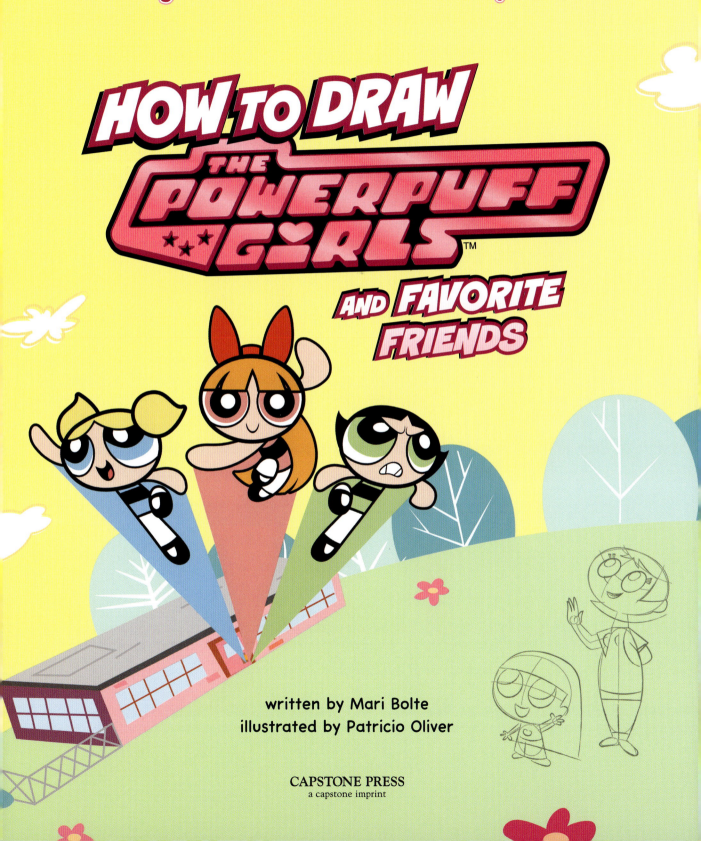

dabblelab

Drawing Adventures with the Powerpuff Girls!

HOW TO DRAW THE POWERPUFF GIRLS AND FAVORITE FRIENDS

written by Mari Bolte
illustrated by Patricio Oliver

CAPSTONE PRESS
a capstone imprint

Published by Capstone Press, an imprint of Capstone.
1710 Roe Crest Drive, North Mankato, Minnesota 56003
capstonepub.com

Copyright © 2024 Cartoon Network.
THE POWERPUFF GIRLS and all related characters and
elements © & ™ Cartoon Network. WB SHIELD: ™ & © WBEI (s24)

All rights reserved. No part of this publication may be reproduced in whole or in part, or stored in a retrieval system, or transmitted in any form or by any means, electronic, mechanical, photocopying, recording, or otherwise, without written permission of the publisher.

Cataloging-in-Publication Data is available on the Library of Congress website.

ISBN: 9781669075554 (hardcover)
ISBN: 9781669075516 (ebook PDF)

Summary: Go on a drawing adventure with the Powerpuff Girls and their friends! Young artists of all abilities will have fun as they learn how to draw the citizens of Townsville alongside Blossom, Bubbles, and Buttercup through easy step-by-step instructions.

Editorial Credits
Editor: Abby Huff; Designer: Hilary Wacholz; Production Specialist: Tori Abraham

Any additional websites and resources referenced in this book are not maintained, authorized, or sponsored by Capstone. All product and company names are trademarks™ or registered® trademarks of their respective holders.

The publisher and the author shall not be liable for any damages allegedly arising from the information in this book, and they specifically disclaim any liability from the use or application of any of the contents of this book.

Printed and bound in China. 5834

TABLE OF CONTENTS

Meet the Powerpuff Girls 4

The Cartoonist's Toolbox 5

Powerpuff Girls to the Rescue! 6

Townsville's Number One Dad 8

Meet and Greet the Mayor 10

Keen on Keane 12

The Robin Next Door 14

Mitch Rocks 16

Blossom's Ballad 18

Batter Up, Buttercup! 20

The New Kid(s) in Town 22

Not What They Seem 24

Blossom, Bubbles, and Buttercup
at the Beach 26

Dream Scheme, Bedtime Routine 28

Read More 32

About the Author 32

About the Illustrator 32

The perfect little girl doesn't exist—

Wait, wait, don't get mad! Let me finish! I was going to say: "The perfect little girl doesn't exist . . . because there are three of them!" Together, Blossom, Bubbles, and Buttercup fight crime and keep the citizens of Townsville safe.

The Powerpuff Girls aren't just superheroes, though. They go to school. They solve mysteries. They even have to take baths and eat their vegetables! Each day brings new friendships and tons of fun.

Enough chitchat. Grab your art supplies and go on an exciting drawing adventure!

THE CARTOONIST'S TOOLBOX

Anyone can put pen to paper and become a cartoonist. Just follow the steps, practice, and have fun! Here are a few tools and tips on how to bring the Powerpuff Girls and their friends to life.

A **pencil** is one of the best drawing tools around! Keep it sharp. Lightly sketch characters first.

Have an **eraser** handy. You're bound to make mistakes, and that's okay! An eraser can also remove lines from earlier steps and polish up your drawing.

Grab a good fine-tip **black marker**. Trace your drawing when it's just how you like. Allow time for the ink to fully dry so it doesn't smudge.

Add a pop of color! **Colored pencils** and **markers** are great options. Bright colors help your finished drawing shine.

POWERPUFF GIRLS TO THE RESCUE!

Once again, the day is saved thanks to the Powerpuff Girls! That's how most of the girls' adventures end. Why wouldn't they? Blossom, Bubbles, and Buttercup each have super speed and super strength. They can fly. They can see in the dark and blast out rays of heat vision. They can even survive in space! WOWZA! When these super sisters work together, there's nothing they can't do.

FACT
Blossom is the leader. She wears a showy bow. Bubbles is sweet. She has super-cute pigtails. Buttercup is tough. Her hair is short—just like her temper!

TOWNSVILLE'S NUMBER ONE DAD

Professor Utonium created a recipe for the perfect little girl. Sugar, spice, and everything nice! Sure, he also dropped some Chemical X in by accident. But it all worked out . . . because Blossom, Bubbles, and Buttercup were born! The Professor loves inventing. If he's not in the lab, he's in the kitchen. (Sadly, his food isn't as good as his science.)

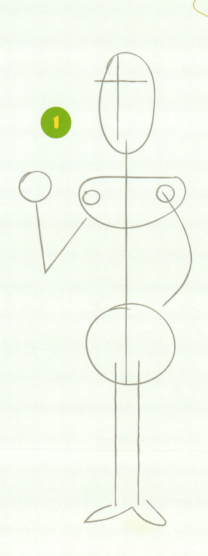

TIP
Pay attention to shapes as you draw characters. The Powerpuff Girls are mostly circles and curved lines. The Professor is more square with sharp edges.

MEET AND GREET THE MAYOR

Oh no! There's an emergency in Townsville! Luckily, the Mayor has a direct line to the most heroic heroes to ever hero. *Ring! Ring!* "Come quick, Powerpuff Girls!" As long as Bubbles doesn't hang up on him, help is (probably) on the way!

TIP
The Mayor likes accessories! Don't forget the buttons on his pointy shoes or the chain on his monocle. Little details make your art pop.

KEEN ON KEANE

Miss Keane is the best—and only—teacher at Pokey Oaks Kindergarten. Good thing she can handle the heat. What's her secret? Let's ask the class. Sorry, Bubbles, it's not a new cat. Fridays are now Food Fight Fridays? Nice try, Blossom. No, those aren't new pants, Buttercup. Stop asking. Maybe Miss Keane's secret is endless patience. Teachers are the real heroes.

FACT
The Powerpuff Girls once set Miss Keane up on a date with Professor Utonium. Sad to say, it didn't work out.

THE ROBIN NEXT DOOR

Friendship isn't always easy. Especially when your new BFFs are off saving the world! Robin Snyder wishes she could spend every afternoon hanging out with the Powerpuff Girls. But their fun keeps getting interrupted by bad guys. Will Blossom, Bubbles, and Buttercup learn to balance work with play? Or will Robin be left alone in the sandbox?

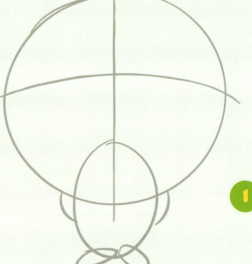

FACT
Robin likes dodgeball and drawing. She lives next door to the Powerpuff Girls.

MITCH ROCKS

Mitch Mitchelson is the bad boy of Pokey Oaks, and he's not going to let anyone forget it. Whether he's messing with the class pet, ruining Bubbles's art projects, or just being a pain, he likes causing a scene. But no matter how naughty Mitch may be, the rowdy boy is still Buttercup's best school friend.

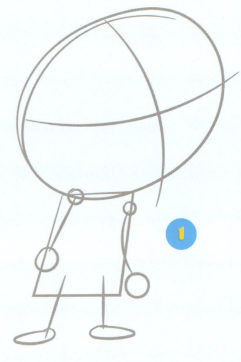

TIP
Write the words on Mitch's shirt in white pencil first. Then carefully add black around the letters, making sure to stay off the white.

BLOSSOM'S BALLAD

Hello? Sorry, Mr. Mayor, you'll have to call back later. Blossom is about to jam! She's got songs about feelings, fighting evil, and wishing for world peace. Now she's taking center stage. And with super speed, going on the road for a world tour is no problem either. Being a hero never sounded so good.

FACT
Blossom's guitar shoots magic waves. They turn gloomy black-and-white things into lively color.

BATTER UP, BUTTERCUP!

Hold on to your hats. Buttercup is up to bat! She can circle the bases at light speed. Good luck to anyone trying to tag her out! This spirited sport takes any and all games seriously. Buttercup is just as tough on a field as she is on crime. Nothing stands in her way.

TIP
Draw Buttercup playing other sports, like hockey, skateboarding, or soccer. How would her powers come in handy?

THE NEW KID(S) IN TOWN

Hey, Pokey Oaks Kindergarten! Meet your new classmate, Mike Believe. He just wants to make a friend. But the one he dreamed up turned out to be a *real* troublemaker. So the Powerpuff Girls had to send Mike's imaginary pal straight to detention. Who will be Mike's best friend now?

TIP
Try drawing Mike a new (and better) imaginary friend.

NOT WHAT THEY SEEM

The city of Townsville. A city full of average people doing average things. The Smiths are like that. This family of four lives right next door to the Powerpuff Girls. But are they *really* as average as they seem? Smile for the camera, Smith family. Your secret's safe—for now.

FACT
Mr. Smith got so tired of his boring life that he became a super-villain! Soon, the rest of his family joined him in his quest for evil.

24

BLOSSOM, BUBBLES, AND BUTTERCUP AT THE BEACH

Between going to school and cleaning up crime, the Powerpuff Girls sure are busy. It's fight, fight, fight in the morning. Spelling tests in the afternoon. Then Professor Utonium's bedtime story in the evening. PHEW! But even heroes need a day off, and the sisters choose to spend it together.

TIP
The girls all have different personalities. Draw what you think each would do on vacation!

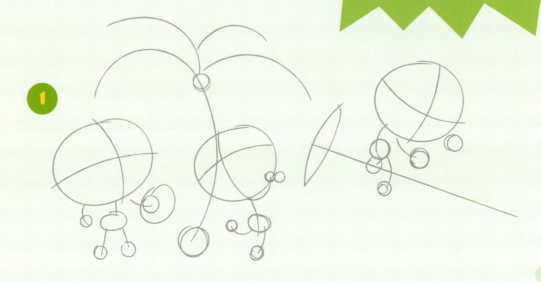

1

DREAM SCHEME, BEDTIME ROUTINE

Shh... Draw as quietly as you can. The sun has set. The citizens of Townsville are turning in. So put on your Powerpuff pajamas because it's time for bed. That is, if Professor Utonium can get this tireless trio to settle down first!

FACT
The Powerpuff Girls and Professor Utonium live at 107 Pokey Oaks South, Townsville, USA.

1

TIP

Feeling like there's too much to draw? Focus first on the characters and the bed. Then fill out the rest of the girls' room.

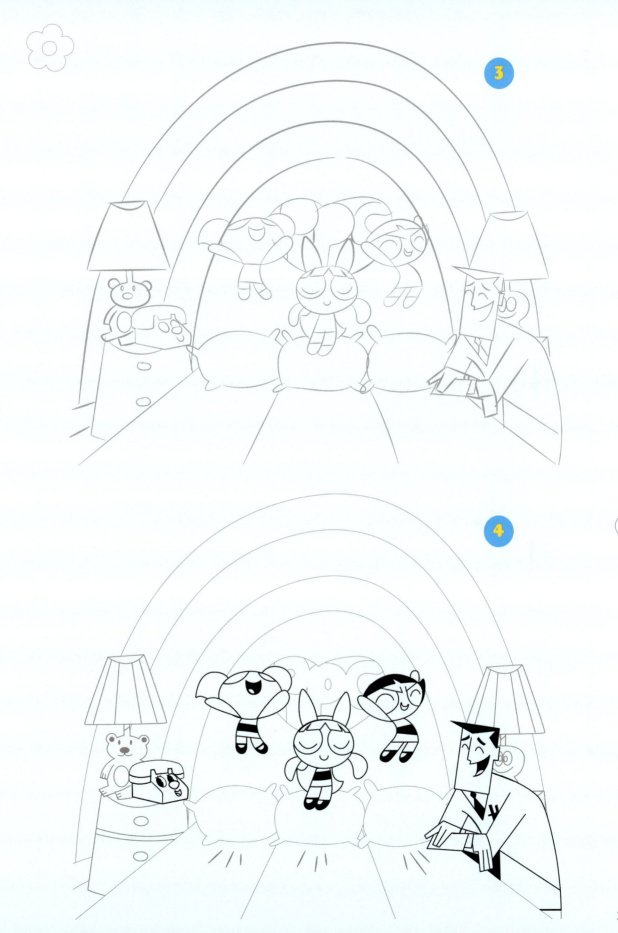

READ MORE

Korté, Steve. *Draw Scooby-Doo!: Monsters, Robots, Aliens, and More.* North Mankato, MN: Capstone Press, 2022.

Nguyen, Angela. *How to Draw Cute Stuff Around the World.* New York: Sterling Children's Books, 2021.

Zoo, Keith. *Drawing Animals: The 7 Essential Techniques & 19 Adorable Animals Everyone Should Know!* New York: Odd Dot, 2021.

ABOUT THE AUTHOR

Mari Bolte is an author and editor of children's books. Whether it's a book on video games, animals, history, science, monsters, or crafts, she's always up for learning new things. (And hoping readers learn something too!) Mari lives in Minnesota with her family and far too many pets.

ABOUT THE ILLUSTRATOR

Patricio Oliver is an illustrator and a graphic designer. A graduate of the University of Buenos Aires, he has worked on books and comics as both an illustrator and writer, focusing on superhero, gender, and diversity themes. He is also a professor of typography and an assistant professor of editorial illustration, and teaches seminars and workshops for various programs.